Robotz to the Rescue!

Adapted by Justin Spelvin
Illustrated by Bill Jankowski
Color by Mark Gallivan

ISBN 0-439-62511-4

12 11 10 9 8 7 6 5 4 3 2 1   4 5 6 7 8/0

Printed in the U.S.A.
First printing, November 2004

SCHOLASTIC INC.

New York   Toronto   London   Auckland   Sydney
Mexico City   New Delhi   Hong Kong   Buenos Aires

On their way home,
the Rescue Heroes Team
spotted a ship in trouble.
"That cruise ship is sinking!"
said Billy Blazes.
"We need to get down there fast!"
The Rescue Heroes Team and their
new robots swooped into action!

"Man overboard!"
shouted Gil Gripper.
"Keep him safe, Nemo."

Jack Hammer and Rivet
went to work patching up
the ship's hull.
"I'm glad you are here,"
said Jack Hammer.
"Two sure is quicker than one!"

"The ship is repaired,"
said Jake Justice.
"Now we can help
these passengers
back on board."
"Roger that!"
10-4 answered.
"Right this way, folks!"

"Oh, no!" Ariel Flyer gasped.
"Where did that tidal wave
come from?"
"Quick!" shouted Billy Blazes.
"We have to lift the ship
before it is too late."

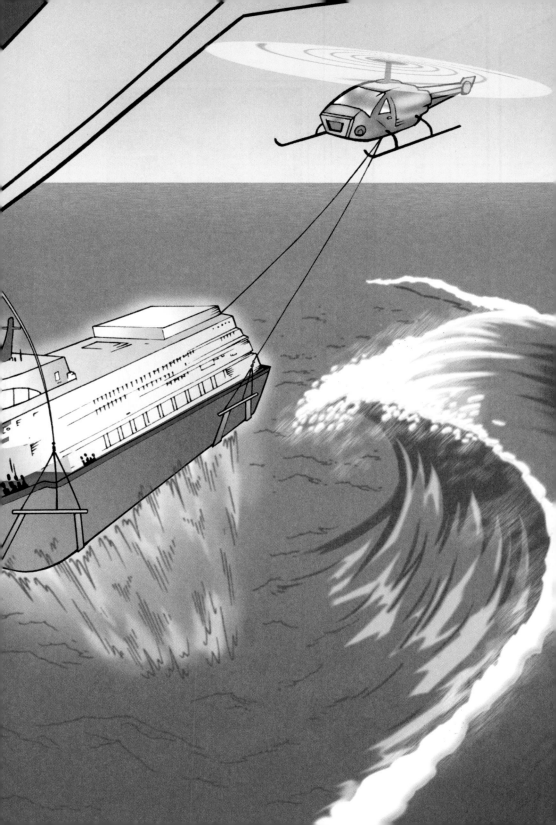

Back at the Command Center,
Warren Waters had bad news.
"Disasters like that tidal wave
are breaking out all over."
"Why?" asked Billy Blazes.
"The earth's core is spinning
the wrong way,"
explained Warren Waters.

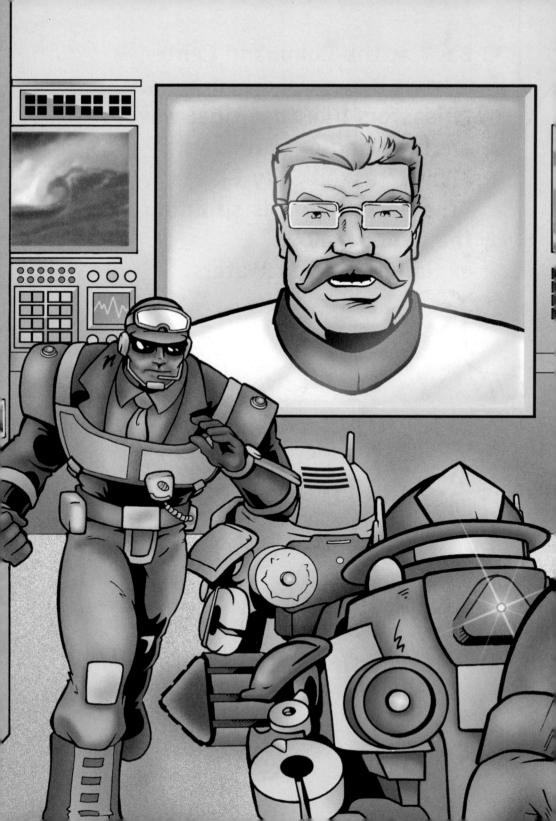

"We need to set off an explosion.
One that is strong enough to force
the earth to spin the right way,"
said Warren Waters.
"But someone would need
to go down there."
"Count us in!" said the team.

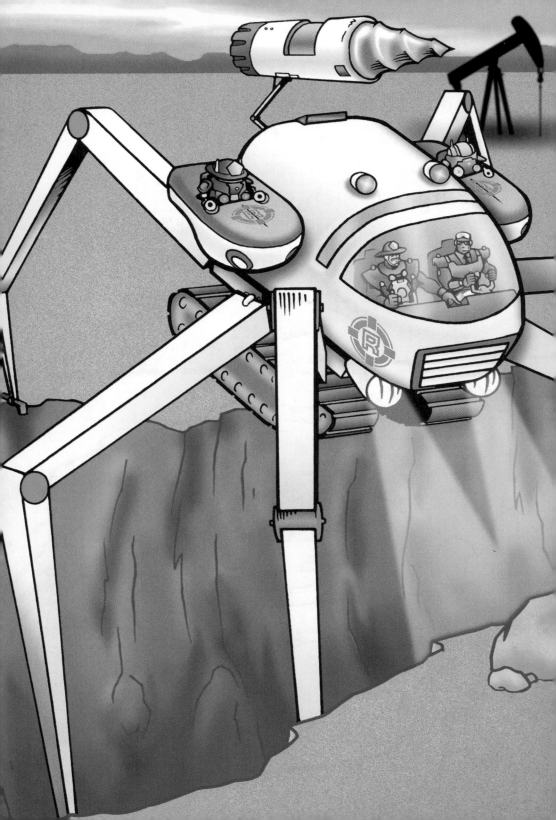

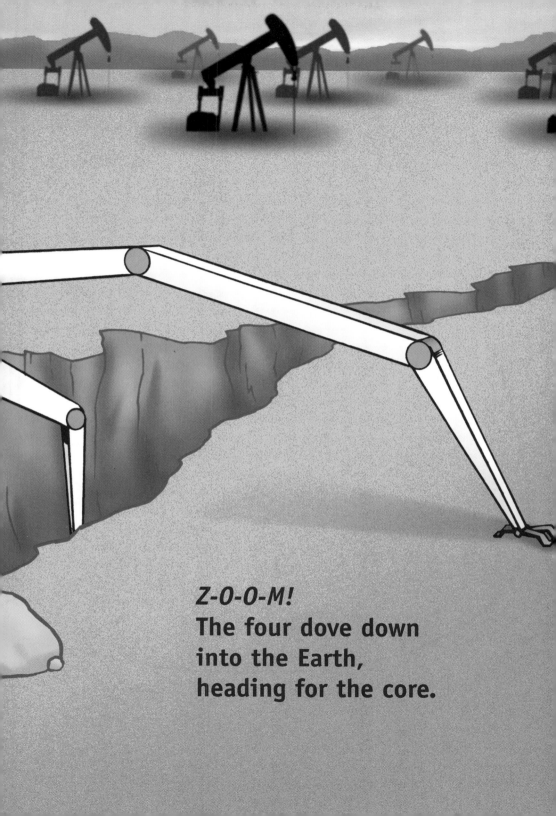

Z-O-O-M!
The four dove down
into the Earth,
heading for the core.

"It is getting hot in here!"
said Jake.
"Too hot for humans,"
added Billy,
"but not Robotz."

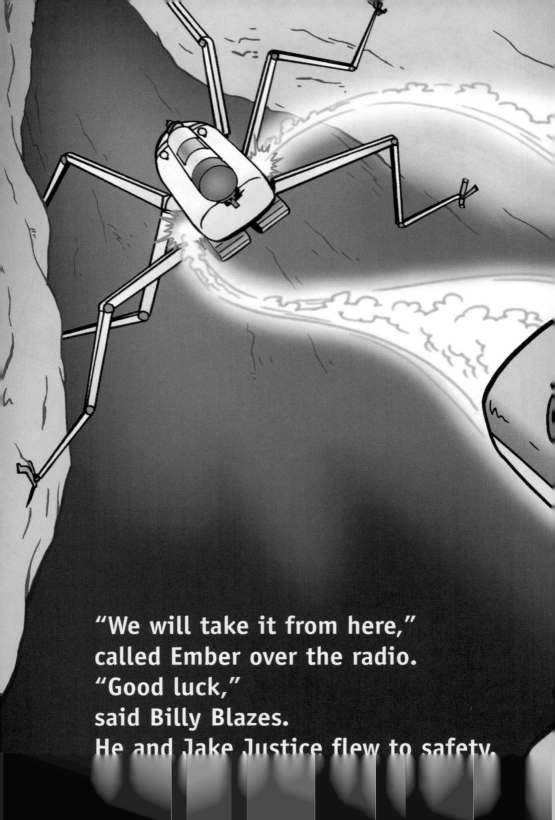

"We will take it from here,"
called Ember over the radio.
"Good luck,"
said Billy Blazes.
He and Jake Justice flew to safety.

"Explosives set,"
reported 10-4.
"We need to get out of here
before the timer runs out,"
said Ember.

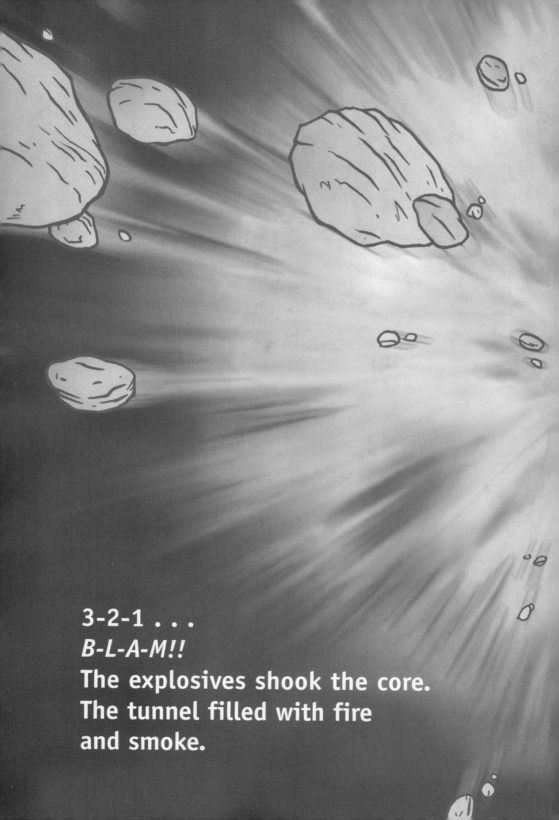

3-2-1 . . .
B-L-A-M!!
The explosives shook the core.
The tunnel filled with fire
and smoke.

"You did it!" reported Pat Pending.
"The core is spinning
the right way again!
Earth is saved!"

"But where are 10-4 and Ember?" asked Jake Justice.

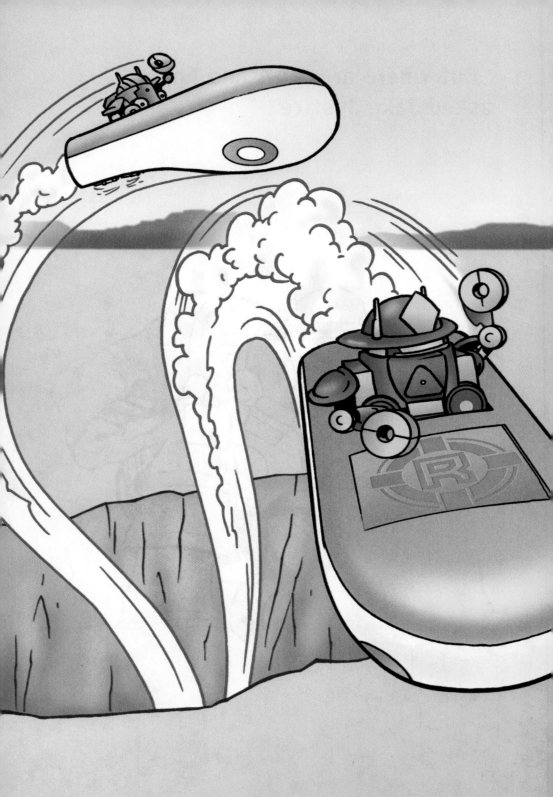

"Whew! They are safe!"
cheered Jake Justice.
"The mission is a success!"
said Billy Blazes.

"We could not have done it without the Robotz!"
said Jake Justice.
"We make a great team!"
said 10-4.